Zachary Goes Groundfishing

On The Trawler *Lucille B.*

Zachary Goes Groundfishing

On The Trawler
Lucille B.

Alice True Larkin

Illustrations by
Abbey Williams

DOWN EAST BOOKS / Camden, Maine

Copyright 1982 by Alice True Larkin
ISBN: 0-89272-084-0
Library of Congress Catalog Card Number: 81-66265
Design: Susan Cramer
Printed in the United States of America

Dedicated to
Troy Charles Hodgdon

Who always thought it was fun
to go down to the docks with his grandmother
and watch the fishermen and the boats.

CONTENTS

SEGUIN LIGHTHOUSE

CHAPTER ONE

GETTING UNDER WAY

Zachary blinked. His eyes were wide open and someone was shaking his shoulder, but he couldn't see anything. Everything was pitch black. Then his bedside lamp clicked on and he could see his mother bending over him.

"Wake up, Zachary," she said. "If you want to go fishing with Captain Richard, you will have to hurry. He will be coming to pick you up in just ten minutes."

It was four o'clock in the morning. Ten-year-old Zachary had never been up that early before. He thought it would be much nicer just to stay snuggled under the warm blankets. Then he remembered how he had teased his mother to let him go fishing with Captain Richard on the trawler *Lucille B.* Sometimes Captain Richard went on long trips to Georges Bank, to catch groundfish — cod, haddock, flounder, and other fish that

1

live on the bottom of the ocean. But today he would be groundfishing just a few miles out from Boothbay Harbor and he had asked Zachary to come along.

Zachary jumped out of bed. He didn't want to miss that trip! His clothes were piled neatly on the chair where he had put them the night before. Captain Richard had told him to bring a warm sweater. Even though it was almost the middle of July, it would be chilly out on the ocean that early in the morning. He pulled the sweater over his head and was just tying his shoes when he heard Captain Richard toot his horn. Zachary ran downstairs.

"I'm all ready!" he shouted. His mother handed him his yellow school slicker. Captain Richard called it "foul weather gear."

"Just in case it rains," she said.

Zachary kissed his mother goodbye and climbed up onto the front seat of the shiny blue pick-up truck. Captain Richard grinned at him.

"Have you got your eyes open yet, Zachary?" he said.

There was no one on the street as they drove through town. Zachary had never seen the stores look so empty and dark. At the fish processing plant where the boats were tied up, a single spotlight on the outside of the building made a pool of warm yellow light on the dock. A smaller light on the wheelhouse lit up the deck of the *Lucille B.* First Mate George and Scotty, the crewman, were already on board. They were getting ready to cast off. George came up to help Zachary climb over the rail.

"Hello, Zachary," he said. "I hear you want to be a fisherman!"

"I'm not sure," Zachary answered. "I want to see what it's like first."

"Well, you come along with us today and see what you think of the job."

It was high tide and the *Lucille B.* was just level with the dock. There was a long, heavy rope, or "line," at each end of the boat. A big loop at the end of the rope was slipped over one of the dock pilings. The two lines held the boat close to the dock but were long enough so it could move up and down with the tide.

Captain Richard ran up a few steps to the wheelhouse, with Zachary right behind him. He flicked a switch and deep down in the bottom of the boat the engines began to rumble and roar.

Captain Richard leaned out the door and signaled

to Scotty that he was ready to get under way. First Mate George and the crewman jumped up onto the dock and lifted the heavy lines off the pilings, then tossed them on deck. Now the boat was starting to move. Zachary was afraid it would leave the men on the dock, but at the last minute, they vaulted nimbly over the rail and the *Lucille B.* moved out into the harbor.

CHAPTER TWO

LEAVING THE HARBOR

There was no one on deck now. Captain Richard turned off the deck light and suddenly there was nothing but darkness and grey mist all around them. It was so dark that Zachary could just barely make out the lobster boats that rocked on their moorings as they passed. They looked like white ghosts in the night. Zachary hoped the *Lucille B.* wouldn't run into any of them. The trawler was plowing straight ahead, but Captain Richard wasn't even looking out the window to see where he was going. Instead, he was looking down into a black box. His eyes were on a screen where a straight white line swept around and around in a circle. There were some white dots on the screen and some larger white blotches. Captain Richard motioned for Zachary to come closer.

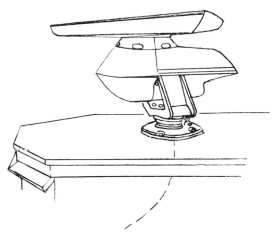

"This is the radar," he said. "It has an antenna that keeps going around, like this white line. The radar sends out an electronic signal, and when it hits something, it bounces back. Then it shows up as a white mark on this screen." He pointed to the white dots. "Those are the lobster boats out there." Captain Richard must have guessed what Zachary was thinking. "I won't run into them," he said, "because I can see them on the radar. Those big white spots are the islands and points of land we are passing." He pointed his thumb at one of them. "We are just going by Squirrel Island now."

"It looks something like a map," Zachary said.

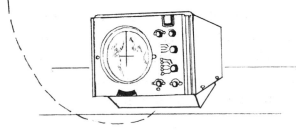

DECCA 36-MILE RADAR

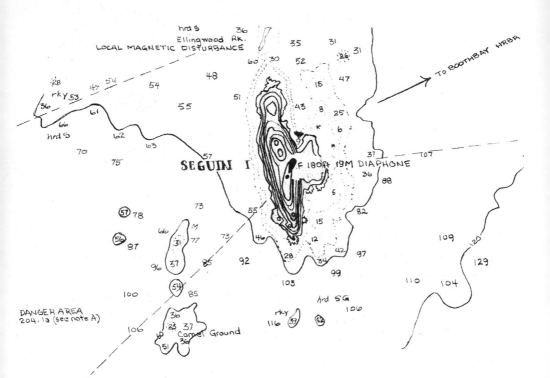

"That's right! What the radar does, really, is to draw a map of everything around us, because I can't see where I'm going in the dark."

"But why do you go when it's dark?" Zachary asked. "Why don't you wait until the sun comes up?"

Just thinking about how early it was made Zachary start to yawn. He clamped his jaws shut to keep the yawn inside. It made his jaws ache but he didn't want Captain Richard to think he minded getting up so early.

"We start out when it's dark," Captain Richard was saying, "so we can get to the fishing grounds before the sun comes up." He turned around to the chart table behind him and unrolled one of the charts that were stacked there, rolled into long white tubes.

"This is where we are now," he said, pointing to the chart, "and this is where we are going. Today we will be fishing near Seguin Light and we will get there just at dawn. The fish start feeding along the bottom when it gets light, and then we can catch them in our nets."

CHAPTER THREE

OUT TO SEA

Before long, the harbor and the lobster boats were far behind them and the radar screen was empty. Captain Richard kept one eye on it, but set his course by a large compass near the wheel. Zachary decided to go out on deck.

"Be careful," Captain Richard warned him. "It will take you a little while to get your sea legs."

Zachary soon found out what he meant. The *Lucille B.* was going faster now and the waves were bigger. The boat climbed to the top of each wave, then the wave dropped out from under it. It pitched and rolled as the bow slapped down into each trough. Zachary had to hang onto things to keep from falling down, and there were some wooden boards, like low fences, that he had to climb over. Captain Richard turned on the deck lights so Zachary could see as he made his way across the deck, then turned them off again once Zachary reached the railing. Now there was only the blackness of the night, the sturdy throb of the engines, and a loud rushing sound as the *Lucille B.* cut through the waves.

Zachary leaned over the railing and looked down. The water didn't look anything like the bright blue ocean sailboats skipped around on when it was a sunny day, and it didn't look like the cool green water where he went swimming at the beach. This water was black, and it looked cold. Some of the dark waves foamed up into white bubbles that chuckled against the side of the boat, then trailed away with a little sigh, as though they hated to be left behind.

The night air whipped back into Zachary's face and he was glad he had worn his sweater. There were no clouds, and overhead he could see the moon and a few bright stars. Then he saw a small white light in the darkness ahead. He turned around and there was another — and another! He knew they couldn't be stars, and they had left the lights of the harbor far behind.

Zachary scrambled back across the deck as fast as he could and rushed up the steps to the wheelhouse.

"Captain Richard!" he panted. "What are all those lights out there?"

"Those are the other fishing boats," Captain Richard laughed. "They are on their way to the fishing grounds, too. There are probably some from Pemaquid, and Bristol, and New Harbor." He boosted Zachary up into the high captain's chair so he could watch the lights out the window. Then he reached overhead and turned on a radio that was fastened to the ceiling. It looked like the citizens' band radio that Zachary's father had in his car. In a few minutes a deep voice boomed through the static.

"Hello there, *Lucille B.* This is Captain Shannon, of the *Brant*."

Captain Richard pressed a button on his mike and answered him. "I have a new man aboard this trip," he said. "His name is Zachary and I think he is going to make a good fisherman."

"Finest kind," Captain Shannon boomed back. "When you get him broken in, perhaps I can get him to work for me."

"Not a chance," Captain Richard laughed. "I want to keep him myself."

The two fishermen chatted back and forth, then some of the other fishing boat captains joined in. Some of them told jokes and one of them sang a little ditty that he had made up about his boat. It was like a big noisy party out in the middle of the ocean! Captain Richard handed the mike to Zachary, but all he could think of to say was "Hi!".

"Hello, Zachary," one of the voices answered. It sounded jolly. "Remember, any time you want a job on a fishing boat, you can sign on with me."

Zachary sat up straighter in the captain's chair. He looked out the window again, hoping to see the sun. When the sun came up, they would be at the fishing grounds, and he was anxious to get started.

CHAPTER FOUR

SHOOTING THE NET

Zachary didn't have long to wait. At first he could see a deep red glow far off in the distance. Then the sun pushed up over the horizon, and suddenly it wasn't dark any more. All around them, looking like toy boats in a big tub, were the other fishing boats they had been talking to. Only no one was talking on the CB now. It was daylight and time to start fishing.

First Mate George came up out of the fo'c's'le with Scotty right behind him. Captain Richard leaned out the window of the wheelhouse and shouted to them to get ready to shoot the net. George nodded. He ran over to a large winch just forward of the wheelhouse and began to push the two levers that operated it. The winch was wound with wire cable, like a stiff rope, which was used to tow the net. The cables were humming across the deck now as the winch began to grind. Zachary ran

down the steps and squeezed himself up flat against the side of the wheelhouse. He wanted to watch the men but didn't want to get in the way.

"Is it all right to stay here?" he shouted up to Captain Richard, who was still leaning out the window.

"That's a good spot, Zachary. Just keep away from the winch. You should be able to see everything from there."

Zachary could see Scotty running to the forward gallows frame. This was a sturdy steel structure shaped like a hangman's gallows, and there was a heavy otter board (or "door") hanging on it. Scotty was getting the door into position to be dropped overboard. There was a second gallows frame on the same side of the boat, near the stern. Captain Richard came down from the wheelhouse to get that door ready.

The trawl net was piled on deck between the two gallows frames. Now Scotty began pushing it overboard. The cod end went first. This was a bag at the end that would hold the fish after they were trapped in the net. It was made of flat, heavy twine, with a drawstring at the bottom that could be untied to let the fish out. The rest of the net was made of bright orange meshes, and it streamed out behind the boat, floating on top of the water. The *Lucille B.* began to turn slowly in the same direction, to keep the trawl away from the boat while the towing cables were run out. Now the cables were really zinging across the deck!

When the trawl net had been run out to its full length, the doors shot overboard with a splash and the net began to sink. In no time at all it was out of sight, and all Zachary could see were the two towing wires disappearing into the water.

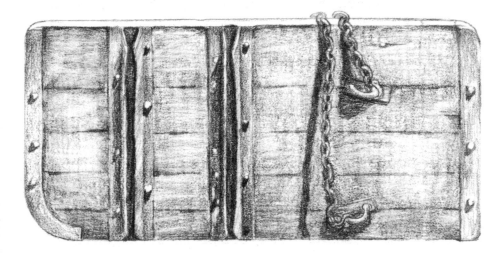

OTTER BOARD

CHAPTER FIVE

THE OTTER TRAWL

The *Lucille B.* had straightened her course now and settled to a steady towing speed. First Mate George stopped the winch and walked back to the wheelhouse. Zachary thought he must have been a fisherman for a long time because he didn't have any trouble keeping his balance. Zachary went to meet him. He thought he was beginning to get his "sea legs," too.

"What are the big doors for?" Zachary asked. "They look terribly heavy."

"I guess they are heavy!" George said. "They are made of oak, two inches thick, and strapped with iron." He stopped and pulled an old envelope out of his shirt pocket. He leaned his back up against the wheelhouse and slid down until he was just as tall as Zachary and propped the envelope on his knee. Then he fished around in his pocket again for a stub of a pencil and began drawing lines on the back of the envelope.

"I'll show you how they work," he said. "These two lines are the towing cables you can see there, running back to the winch." Then he sketched in the net, like a big funnel, making crosshatches on the paper to show the meshes, and labeling the parts. "This is called an 'otter trawl.' "

He drew a black rectangle for each door, with lines to show how it was attached between the trawl and the towing cables.

"These are the doors. The real name for them is 'otter boards' but we call them doors. They drag along the bottom like a playing card on edge and hold the net down. The water acts like wind on a kite, pushing them apart and keeping the net spread. The doors have to be made rugged because they take an awful beating riding over the rocks."

Zachary whistled. Now he understood why the doors looked so heavy and why they had been so scarred up. He looked back at the drawing on the envelope. First Mate George was drawing little round circles in a row along the wide end of the otter trawl, at the top.

"Now you've got the doors holding the net down on the bottom and spreading it apart," he said, "but you've got to have something to hold the mouth open or it would just drag along like an old rag and wouldn't catch any fish."

"What are those little circles?" Zachary asked.

"Those are floats on the headrope, to hold the top

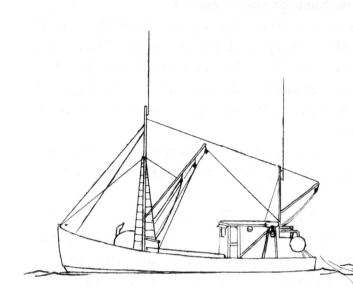

edge of the net up in the water." George pointed to a spare trawl net piled on the deck nearby. "You can see some of them there." Zachary looked where he was pointing. He could see some round metal balls on the net.

Now First Mate George was drawing more circles on the footrope at the bottom of the trawl. "This is the roller frame." He pointed to the spare net again. "The bobbins — the big ones there that look like iron basketballs — roll along the bottom like wheels and help keep the net from getting caught on every little thing. Of course, they bounce around some, but they hold the net down. Those black rubber discs that look like pieces cut out of old automobile tires are used as spacers between the bobbins and on each side." He added some more little circles to the footrope on the drawing. "Now, if we were fishing on mud bottom, instead of rocks," he added, "we wouldn't use those. We would have a piece of chain looped along the footrope instead."

OTTER BOARD

BOBBINS

HEADROPE FLOATS

COD END

FOOTROPE

ROLLER FRAME

Zachary nodded. He could see the roller frame under the spare net. Then he noticed something else. It looked like an old mop and was all different colors. "What is that?" he asked. "It looks like little pieces of rope, all unraveled."

"That's about what it is, I guess," First Mate George said. It's called the 'chafing gear,' or 'chafer,' and it goes underneath the cod end. It helps to keep the twine from chafing, or wearing through." He added a few scratches to the cod end to show the chafing gear. Zachary studied the drawing on the envelope. "It looks like a big hungry mouth that gobbles up fish," he said.

First mate George handed the envelope to Zachary and stood up again. His eyes were crinkled at the corners and he was smiling.

"You are a pretty smart kid," he said. "That is exactly how it works."

CHAPTER SIX

LOOKING FOR FISH

Zachary felt good. He climbed up to the wheel-house again to see what Captain Richard was doing.

"I'm looking for a good bunch of fish," Captain Richard told him. He was watching another electronic instrument next to the radar which he called a fish finder, or echo sounder. Instead of a glass screen it had a roll of white paper that kept moving while a pointed marker drew black lines on it.

"What do the lines mean, Captain Richard?" Zachary asked.

"Well, this black line along the bottom shows the ocean floor. See, here it is quite smooth, but back there are some sharp peaks that are probably reefs or large rocks."

He pointed to some small black dots on the paper. "Those are fish," he said, "swimming down there near the bottom. When there is a school of fish — a lot of fish swimming together — it looks like a big black smudge on the paper." He turned to another instrument.

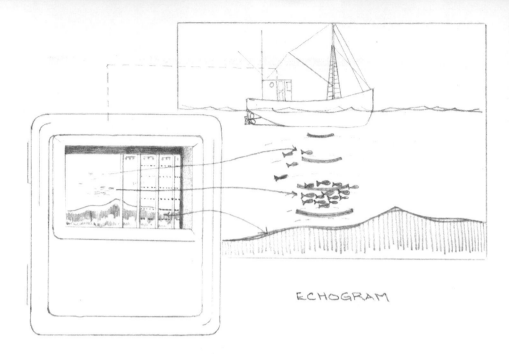

ECHOGRAM

"This is the sonar. It works a lot like the radar, but the antenna is under water. The sonar draws a map of the ocean floor up ahead and on each side of the boat. It shows me if there is anything there, like a reef or an old shipwreck, that would rip up our nets."

Zachary looked out the window. He could see the other fishing boats spread out across the water. They were looking for fish, too. The boats sailed slowly in one direction for several miles, then made a sweeping turn and came back again. Captain Richard turned on the CB and talked to some of the men. Nobody seemed to be having any luck. Captain Shannon's jolly voice came over the CB. "I've seen more fish in my cucumber patch!" he said.

CHAPTER SEVEN

BREAKFAST IN THE FO'C'S'LE

Captain Richard was watching the fish finder. There were only a few scattered black dots on it.

"When I find a good-sized school of fish," he said, "We'll chase them with the net and you can see how it is done."

Zachary kept his eyes on the paper, too. He hoped they would find a school of fish soon. He was also thinking about his stomach. It was really beginning to feel empty.

Just then, First Mate George came in the door with a plate of scrambled eggs, fried potatoes, and bacon, with four slices of buttered toast piled on top. He handed the plate to Captain Richard and set a thick mug of steaming hot coffee down in front of him.

"You can come down in the fo'c's'le and have breakfast with us, Zachary," he said. Zachary grinned at Captain Richard and hurried out the door after him. They didn't have to ask him twice!

Zachary followed First Mate George to the bow of the boat and down a ladder into a room full of noise and light, and a lot of nice breakfast smells. The fo'c's'le was where the men lived when they were not busy working on deck. There were bunks along the sides, squeezed in so close together that you would bump your head if you

sat up straight. On one side there was a small table with benches, like a restaurant booth. Zachary slid onto one of the benches with First Mate George.

Scotty was cooking bacon on a tiny gas stove. It looked like a regular stove except that it had a railing around the top edge. There was a railing around the table, too, and after Scotty had fetched Zachary a glass of milk, he pulled out a wooden pin in the wall that made sure the refrigerator door stayed shut.

Zachary could feel the boat moving under him although it was a fair day with just a little breeze. Then he closed his eyes and tried to imagine what it would be like in a storm.

"I'll bet I know why the railings are there," he thought. "They are to keep the pots and pans and dishes from flying off when the sea is rough!"

Scotty piled his plate with bacon and eggs and fried potatoes. Then he put a big stack of toast on the table. The men told Zachary he would have to eat up if he was going to be a fisherman. They talked and laughed while they ate. The men ate fast but didn't seem to be in a hurry to leave the table. Scotty turned on a portable radio and listened to the news and weather.

"There isn't much to do while we are making the first tow," First Mate George explained. "Sometimes we tow the net for an hour or two, looking for fish or it might be only twenty minutes. Later on, after we have hauled back, we will be plenty busy cleaning the fish while we make another tow. But now we can just sit around and be lazy!"

The news was over and the radio began to play rock-and-roll. Scotty turned it up louder and kept time with his head and his heels while he cleared the table and washed the dishes. Zachary offered to help dry the dishes and put them away. The cups went on narrow shelves with a railing in front of them, and everything else went in a cupboard with stout doors.

"We'll have this place shipshape in no time," Scotty said.

CHAPTER EIGHT

HAULING BACK

After the galley — which is what they called the kitchen — was all "shipshape" Zachary climbed the ladder and went back to the wheelhouse. Captain Richard was watching a school of fish that was a solid mass on the fish finder.

"I think we got 'em," he said. The men had come up on deck, too, and he signaled to them to start hauling the net back. First Mate George ran to the winch and the cables began to hum. Scotty and Captain Richard hooked the doors to the gallows frames again as they came out of the water, and in a few moments, Zachary could see the orange meshes of the trawl. He hadn't noticed any seagulls around the boat before, but now there seemed to be hundreds of them. They wheeled and soared over the boat, wailing their mournful cries. Now the cod end was coming up. It was bulging with silvery, sparkling fish. The seagulls screeched and dived at it. Some of them landed on the cod end and began picking at the fish through the mesh.

The men worked fast to pull the net in over the side of the boat. The "quarter ropes" pulled the mouth of the trawl net together, and a winch helped bring the roller frame aboard. Then the men pulled the main body of the twine in by hand. The "gilson", a hook on a straight line that passes through a block, hoisted the heavy cod end on deck.

Scotty loosened the drawstring on the cod end and the fish slid out, splattering drops of water in all directions. Zachary jumped back. Fish were thrashing all over the deck and the men were slipping and sliding knee deep in them. Zachary had never seen so many fish.

The trawl net was put overboard again for another tow and Captain Richard went back up to the wheelhouse. Scotty and First Mate George were wearing hip boots that were turned down below the knee in wide cuffs. They grabbed the cuffs of their boots and pulled them all the way up their legs. Then they got down on their hands and knees and began sorting fish.

CHAPTER NINE

CLEANING THE CATCH

Now Zachary found out what all those wooden fences were. Captain Richard called them "checkerboards" and they divided the midsection of the deck into small pens, or "pounds." Codfish with big heads and even bigger mouths went into one pen. Flounder, and "dabs" went in another. These were flat, like a frisbee, and had two curious little eyes on stalks. There was a section for haddock, and for another large fish with a long whisker at each side of its head.

"Is that a hake?" Zachary asked. He had seen his mother buy one at the store for his father's favorite dish of corned hake, pork scraps, and potato.

"That's right!" Scotty nodded. He picked up a very ugly fish that had such a big mouth there wasn't much room left for his tail. "Monkfish tails are good to eat, too," he said.

CODFISH

FLOUNDER

DAB

HADDOCK

HAKE

SOLE

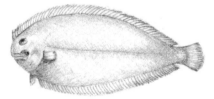

SCULPIN

MONKFI

There were some very small fish that the men threw overboard. "The holes in the mesh are made big enough to let the small fish swim through them to get away," First Mate George said, "but some of them get crowded down into the cod end."

Then he picked up a big sculpin and tossed it over the side. A swarm of seaguls pounced on it before it hit the water.

"Those fellows are just too ugly looking to eat!" he chuckled.

After the fish were separated, the men started cleaning them with long sharp knives.

The "round" fish have to be gutted right away," Scotty said, picking up a big codfish. He made a quick slash across the fish's undersides, just below the gills, then another slash down its belly. He pulled out the entrails and gills and tossed them over the side of the boat. Instantly, a horde of seagulls came shrieking after them.

"We have to feed the gulls," Scotty laughed. "They are the scavengers of the sea and keep the place cleaned up. I guess you could call them our garbage collectors."

After the cod, hake, and haddock were gutted, the men washed them off thoroughly with a hose that sucked water up from the sea. Then Scotty lifted the large hatch cover over the fish hold and placed it carefully on the deck. He winked at Zachary.

"Don't ever turn a hatch cover upside down on a boat," he said. "It is terrible bad luck."

"Is that a superstition?" Zachary asked.

"Yes. Fishermen have a lot of them. Some of the younger fellows don't pay much attention to them, but no one would turn a hatch cover upside down!"

Zachary watched the men pack the fish in the hold and spread chipped ice over them to keep them fresh. The "flatfish" — flounders, sole, and dabs — went into the hold just as they had come out of the water.

"We don't clean these," Scotty explained. "We don't even wash them off, but we try to pack them with the white side up. They keep better that way."

After awhile, Zachary began to feel sleepy. He covered his mouth with both hands, but this time he couldn't hold back a yawn.

"Why don't you go down in the fo'c's'le and take a nap," First Mate George suggested. "We probably won't haul back again for an hour or so."

Zachary didn't protest. There was a heavy wool blanket on the bunk that smelled of the bacon they had had for breakfast. It smelled a little bit like fish, too. Zachary took off his shoes and crawled under the blanket. He curled up on his side, but the boat rolled back and forth and kept knocking him over. Finally, he turned over on his stomach. Then the motion of the boat was soothing, like swinging in his back yard. In a few minutes, he was fast asleep.

CHAPTER TEN

MENDING THE NET

When Zachary woke up he could hear the towing cables humming overhead, and when he got up on deck the men were just bringing the cod end aboard. This time there were no fish in it. Instead, there was a huge jagged piece of wood.

"It looks like a piece of the hull from an old shipwreck," George said. There were hundreds of tiny holes and tunnels in the wood. "Look at those worm holes!" he said. "You can tell she has been on the bottom for a long time."

Captain Richard came down from the wheelhouse to see how badly the trawl net was torn. "Well! I guess we got rimracked that time!" he said.

The men removed the old timber carefully, but it had already ripped great holes in the trawl. All the fish that had been in the net had escaped out the holes. Captain Richard looked at his watch and then looked up at the sky. There were some black clouds building up in the east.

"It looks like it is going to blow before long," he said. "We might as well head back." He started up the steps to the wheelhouse. "If you have an extra needle," he called back to First Mate George, "you can teach Zachary how to mend. If he wants to be a fisherman, that's a good place to start."

Scotty lifted the net up with the gilson so they could get at the holes, while George went to get a handful of needles and a big spool of twine. He showed Zachary how to fill the needles by winding the twine around a cut-out place in the center. Then he began to mend. How his fingers flew!"

"Watch me," he said. He showed Zachary how to hold the needle, and step by step, how to make the knots. After a few tries, Zachary could do it by himself, although his meshes were not as straight and even as theirs. First Mate George found some small places for Zachary to mend while he and Scotty worked on the biggest holes.

"Sometimes," Scotty grumbled, "I think a fisherman spends more time mending than he does fishing." Zachary laughed. He thought mending the net was fun, but he liked it better when the cod end came up full of fish instead of holes.

CHAPTER XI

BACK HOME AGAIN

It didn't seem long before they were back in the harbor again. The men had worked right through the noon hour, but would go home to eat when they docked. Then they would come back to unload the fish.

Zachary leaned against the rail. He could see the fish plant and the dock getting closer. The *Lucille B.* was headed straight for the dock and Zachary held his breath. He though they were going to crash right into it. At the last minute, Captain Richard put the engines in reverse and the big trawler eased gently up to the dock.

It was the same dock they had left that morning, but now it was almost low tide and the dock was higher than the boat. Scotty and First Mate George scrambled up a long ladder that was built flat up against the side of the dock. When they had made the boat fast to the dock, Zachary climbed up the ladder, too. Captain Richard handed a plastic bag up to him. He had put a hake and a couple of haddock in it.

"Here's something for your supper, Zachary," he said. "The next time you come with us we will get you some boots and teach you how to clean fish."

Zachary grinned. He was clutching a needle and a piece of old trawl netting that Scotty had given him to practice on.

"I'll be seeing you, Captain Richard," he said. "Thank you for taking me fishing."

CAPTAIN RICHARD McLELLAN was born in Damariscotta, Maine in 1949. At the age of 19, he was the captain of the *Lucille B.* and was the youngest trawler captain on the Maine coast. After selling the *Lucille B.* in 1977, he purchased the 76-foot steel trawler, *Sea Bring*. He is presently fishing with the *Sea Bring* out of Boothbay Harbor, Maine.

The *Lucille B.* is a 55-foot wooden trawler with a 16½-foot beam and 7½-foot draft. She was built in 1954 at the Lash Brothers shipyard in Friendship, Maine. She is typical of the eastern-rigged side trawler popular with New England fishermen before 1960, but now being gradually replaced by the western-rigged, or stern, trawler. The distinguishing feature of the side trawler is that both gallows frames are on the same side of the vessel, with the wheelhouse on the stern and the fo'c's'le forward.

The *Lucille B.* was owned and operated by Captain Richard McLellan of Boothbay Harbor from 1968 to 1976. In 1973, the boat was converted to a stern-rigged trawler, although the wheelhouse was not moved. The *Lucille B.* was sold in 1977 to John Vasque of Provincetown, Massachusetts. He changed her name to *Gale.*

GLOSSARY

Block: A pulley, used for lifting heavy objects.

Bobbins: Heavy iron balls, used on the footrope to hold the net down on the bottom and to help it travel over rocks.

Bow: The front, or forward, section of a boat.

Cable: A heavy rope, usually made of steel.

Chafer: A mat made from pieces of twine or netting, used to keep the cod ends from wearing through. Also called **Chafing Gear**.

Chart: A map of the ocean or coastline, giving the depth of the water and showing navigational markers and dangers.

Checkerboards: Wooden boards used to divide the mid-portion of the deck into sorting pens for the fish.

Cod End: The end of the trawl which holds the fish. It is usually made of stouter twine and has a drawstring, or clip, at the end which can be opened to release the fish. Sometimes called **Bag**.

Dabs: A type of flounder or flatfish.

Dock: Usually a wooden structure built on poles and extending out into the water. A place for boats to tie up. Also called a **Wharf** or a **Pier**.

Doors: Common name for **Otter Boards.** These are heavy, door-shaped devices, usually made of wood and strapped with iron. They are attached to each side of the trawl and ride along the ocean floor on edge, protected from rocks by heavy iron "shoes." The weight of the doors holds the net on the bottom of the ocean. The force of water pushing against them as they are towed spreads them apart and keeps the trawl net open.

Dragger: Another name for **Trawler.** Common in Maine and New England.

Dragging: Another name for **Trawling.**

Echo Sounder: An electronic instrument used to locate fish under water. Also called a **Fish Finder.**

Finest Kind: A fisherman's slang, meaning "very good."

Fish Finder: Another name for **Echo Sounder.**

Fish Hold: A section of the vessel — usually amidships on a side trawler — where the fish are kept packed in ice until they can be unloaded.

Flat Fish: Fish that are wide and flat, like a pancake, with eyes on top. Includes flounder, sole, and rays.

Floats: Hollow metal or plastic balls attached to the head rope of an otter trawl to hold it up in the water.

Fo'c's'le: The room or area on a boat where the crew lives. On a small vessel, it may include the galley. A contraction of **Forecastle.**

Footrope: A heavy rope on the bottom edge of a trawl's wide opening. It carries the bobbins, or roller frame.

Foul Weather Gear: Rubberized or plastic waterproof clothing. Usually bright yellow or orange, which can be seen easily if a man falls overboard.

Galley: The cooking, or kitchen, area on a boat.

Gallows Frame: A stout metal frame, shaped like an upside-down U. The trawl net is towed from the gallows frames, and the otter board is suspended on it, when not in use.

Gilson: A straight line with a hook on one end.

Ground Fish: Fish that live and feed near the bottom of the ocean.

Groundfishing: Dragging a net along the bottom of the ocean to catch bottom-feeding fish. Also called **Bottom Fishing.**

Hatch: An opening in the deck of a boat, giving access to space below.

Hatch Cover: The lid over a hatch.

Head Rope: A heavy rope attached to the top edge of the trawl's meshes at the wide opening.

Line: A rope, or cable.

Make Fast: To moor a boat, or tie something securely.

Mesh: The open spaces between the cords, or twine, used to make a net. Also the twine around the spaces.

Needle: A pointed shuttle, made of wood or plastic, used for knitting or mending nets.

Net: A bag-shaped trapping device made up of twine meshes. Also referred to as **Twine.**

Otter Board: See **Door.**

Otter Trawl: A type of trawl used for bottom, or ground-fishing. It is shaped like a funnel.

Pilings: Heavy timbers or posts driven into the ground under water, and used to support a dock or a building.

Quarter Ropes: Two stout ropes that are run through rings on the headrope to the footrope. Pulled by a winch on deck, they close the mouth of the trawl when hauling back and lifting the bobbins, or roller frame, so that the fish are trapped in the net.

Radar: An electronic instrument that locates objects above the water.

Rimracked: A fisherman's slang for getting his net torn up.

Roller Frame: Hard rubber disks and metal bobbins attached to the footrope of a trawl. Their weight holds the net down and the bobbins roll over the rocks like wheels as the net is dragged along the ocean bottom.

School of Fish: A large number of fish, usually the same kind, swimming close together.

Ship Shape: Neat and tidy.

Sonar: An electronic instrument that locates objects under the water.

Stern: The back, or after, section of a boat.

Towing Cables: Heavy wire cables wound on a deck winch and attached to the trawl net.

Trawl, Trawl Net: A net used for fishing.

Trawler: A boat or vessel used for fishing done by towing a net. Also called **Dragger** or **Beam Trawler**.

Twine: Stout cord or thread used in the meshes of a net. Sometimes the net itself.

Wharf: Another name for **Dock**.

Wheelhouse: A small building or room on a boat which contains the steering mechanism, compass, and all the electronic equipment. It is usually built high and has windows all around it.

Winch: A round drum with mechanical or hydraulic power, and wound with rope or cable. The **Trawl Winch** is used to lower the trawl to the bottom and haul it up. Smaller winches are used for various other hoisting jobs.